A LUCKY TURN?

TURN ONE

The day began just like any other. Frank, a 32-year old, 6ft 6in, overweight and balding security guard was being woken by the shrill of his alarm clock. It was dark, it was raining; he hated this time of the day... He felt like a drone that no one knew even existed.

His wife of 13 years, Claire, beside him, rolled over and muttered 'Idiot,' under her breath. She then let out a low rumbling fart. He felt great.

Sat on the edge of the bed, Frank bent over to put his socks on. He could feel his ass cheeks open slightly and, magically, the bottom sheet of the bed had a kiss leaving a lovely stain behind him.

'Crap,' he muttered then laughed to himself.

' Shut the fuck up and get to work,' said Claire 'and don't come back!. '

'That suits me fine' snarled Frank. He put his other sock on and left a deeper stain. She is going to go nuts, he thought to himself. Another grin crossed his face.

He stood up and reached for his underpants. He gave them a sniff to check how they were doing. Only a slight smell of urine from the night before, they were good for a few more days yet. Hopping slightly to get his legs in, as he reached for his jeans that were hanging on the back of the chair, he leaned forward letting out a high pitched squeaky wet one.

'Will you get the fuck out of here, you idiot!' screamed Claire.

'Love you too, baby,' replied Frank. He grabbed his Welsh rugby top and headed off to the bathroom. After a quick brush of his teeth and a wash, he headed off downstairs.

Breakfast was a bowl of cereals, no sugar and low-fat milk. Mm lovely, he thought, this diabetes was getting him down, but who would want to listen to his moaning?

The stiff front door screeched as he opened it and made his way down the damp dark path to his rusty 15-year old Volvo.

The car started the first time. Wow, he thought, miracles will never cease.

On went the lights, radio, and the blower, the windscreen slowly cleared, and the news came on. It was 4 a. m. The same 4 a. m. as it was yesterday and the day before and the week before and the month before.

'I am like a fucking robot,' he muttered to himself, his hands tightened on the steering wheel as he rocked back and forth. There has to be more than this, he thought.

His eyes started welling up, as Bob Dylan came on the radio. Buckets of rain, one of his favourite songs.

The car was put into drive. Frank wiped his eyes and started his hour-long drive to work.

To make himself feel better, he thought about the special delivery today at work. All that gold arriving for the minting of the commemorative coins. Something different, at least.

He was also looking forward to the weekend – all of it to himself. Claire worked for an insurance company that did a lot of work's weekends away for their employees. 'The pay's good too,' his best friend, Charlie, a director at the company, had said to Claire.

On the way, he stopped to get some bread and a lotto ticket from the garage, toast for dinner and toast for tea. He had to eat regularly to stop himself from passing out but keep his weight down at the same time. Eighteen grams of carbs a slice, what a load of crap.

He walked through the automatic sliding double doors.

'Morning Tony, just a loaf today and my lucky numbers on the lotto please. Oh, and a pack of 10 Sterling Super Kings. '

He had known Tony for over 3 years. A young Italian who worked the dead shift on account of his terrible acne and fear of women.

'Morning Franky boy, how they hanging?'

'Close to the floor thanks for asking,' replied Frank.

'You can have this loaf I was going to chuck it out last night but thought of you. You have to be the tightest bloke I know.

tighter than a duck's arse!' Tony's laugh was like a weasel coughing on speed.

'Cheers, big ears,' said Frank.

He took his cigarettes and loaf, turned around and came face to face with an angel.

The shock of seeing someone so beautiful took his breath away and he took a step back. The middle of the sweet counter hit the back of his knees and he tipped over like a sack of shit, falling on his loaf of bread and landing with his head under the angel's short skirt.

'Oh my God, are you alright?' she said.

Frank blurted out, 'I have died and gone to heaven.' He blushed and told himself to shut up, as he lifted himself off the floor he brushed against her huge bust. 'Oh shit, sorry. That was an accident, honest.' His eyes were fixed on her cleavage.

'Well, you don't look sorry,' she said and placed her outspread fingers on her chest.

'Sorry. Sorry, I didn't mean to stare. Bloody hell, how embarrassing is this?' He ran his fingers through what he had left of his hair and closed his eyes.

'Don't worry about it?' she said. 'I love looking at them too. ' With that she pushed them even further out.

Frank could not believe what he was seeing. Tony was standing with his mouth open and hadn't blinked since the girl had walked in.

'I have got to go,' said Frank. 'I'm going to be late.'

The loaf of bread started spilling out on the floor. This was more like it, he thought. I have loads of luck. He laughed. All of it bad. He smiled at the temptress and gave her a wink.

'Your luck's in today,' she said. 'After I get my pint of milk, you can come to mine for a coffee and crumpets.'

POLICE

Frank's first thoughts were about his underpants. Then his wife.

Tony started coughing violently, he'd managed to swallow his chewing gum and was going a purple shade of red.

Frank threw what was left of his loaf of bread in the air and skidded around the counter like a whippet. His first aid training kicked in and gave Tony the biggest slap on the back he could muster. Tony's belly hit the panic button under the counter, the shutters came down and the police were called remotely.

Tony was still gasping for air, then Frank picked him up and shook him like a rag doll. Tony passed out momentarily when his eye struck the 'pay her' sign, he opened his eyes to the sight of a huge bosom and a soft voice telling him to 'cough. cough...'

He did and out flew the chewing gum.

It did not take long for Tony to catch his breath.

'What the hell were you trying to do. squeeze me to death?' he shouted at Frank.

'I just saved your life,' replied Frank and gave him a clip across the back of his head.

'Actually, I saved you. but then I am a nurse. '

Both the men looked at her and said in unison, 'You're a nurse dressed like that?!'

'I've been out. and before you ask my name, it's Sherry. Come here and let me have a look at that eye. '

Tony leaned forward over the counter and kept his gaze on two of the best assets he had ever seen, when he received a bigger clip to the back of the head from Frank.

'Will you two boys cut it out? This eye needs attention, where do you keep the superglue? And I will need some tissue or wipes. '

By now the blood was covering half of Tony's face.

'I will get it; I know where everything is in this place. ' Frank had spent many hours wandering the isles to keep out of the way of his once loving wife. He was back within a shot. 'Here you go nurse Sherry, glue and tissues. Ha. Sounds like a carry-on film. '

'Easy tiger,' replied Sherry.

She turned her glance towards Tony 'close your eye and keep still a moment, I'm just going to clean you up. ' She wiped the blood from around the gash and applied a small spot of glue. 'And... there. All done. '

'What the hell have you done?' squealed Tony.

Sherry had managed to glue the tissue to his eyebrow. As he blinked, he looked like a startled king penguin.

Frank glanced at his watch. 'Shit, have you seen the time? I need to get going. I can't believe I'm not going to take up your offer of coffee and crumpets, Sherry, but then again, my missus might have something to say about that. Come on Tony, open these doors, I will catch you tomorrow.'

Tony stared at him. 'Get these doors open! Have you seen my fucking eye?'

Frank gave out one of his booming laughs. Sherry was doubled over. Then gravity took over and both her breasts fell out Frank and Tony looked at each other then back at Sherry. The three of them were like a group of school kids rolling in the isles.

'Hang on, what about your fags and lottery ticket? And you will have to buy another loaf of bread, you need to eat!'

'You're right again, Tony Baloney. Get those shutters up while I get the loaf.'

Tony reset the alarm and pushed the release button on the doors. Nothing happened. He tried again, and the button fell off.

'Shit,' he said. 'Huston, we have a problem.'

'Right Tony, this will do,' said Frank after running to the bread section and back. 'And don't forget my lottery ticket. Make it snappy, I have to get to work. The Royal Mint won't look after itself, you know'.

Sherry's eyes narrowed.

'I need to ring the alarm people; these doors aren't moving, and the knob just fell off!'

'Stop messing about, you numpty, I have to get going. I'm sure Sherry has to get out of here too. Am I right Sherry?'

'Yes. But I don't have anything to rush home to, I was hoping you were going to come with me.'

Frank was getting a bit uneasy with the forward Sherry. Why on earth was a woman like this showing him any interest let alone trying to get him into bed? He thought about his shift today and the special delivery. Is this a way to keep me from my shift? I doubt it, he thought, he was going to be nowhere near that part of the plant.

'Frank. Frank. What the hell are you doing? You're away with the fairies again,' said Tony.

'I was thinking... about stuff. Listen, get these doors open. I have to get going.'

'I am trying to get through to the twenty-four-hours alarm company. Twenty-four hours my arse. There's a recorded message saying they will be open at 9 am. That's nearly five hours away!'

'Have you got a kettle in here? And a toaster? I'm starving,' said Sherry.

'There's one out the back, white with eight sugars for me please. But don't stir it, I don't like it sweet.' Tony gave his stock answer. For some reason he always thought that was funny.

'Hang on a minute, I need to get to work!' shouted Frank. 'I am on my last warning.'

He ran towards the door and gave it a rattle. There was no way it could be shifted, after all it was built to stop ram raids.

'Honestly, this will be the last straw. No job. The missus will leave, not that I will worry about her too much, but I need my job.'

'You need to calm down, big boy. I will make you a cuppa. What you want, tea or coffee, black or white?' asked Sherry.

Frank started feeling a little bit sick, he knew he had to get out of there and quick. 'Listen, Tony, I have to get out of here!'

'Listen, Frank, we are not going anywhere! The shutters are down, the doors are on lockdown. You better ring your boss and tell them the news that you are not going to work until gone nine.'

TEA COFFEE AND TOAST

The three of them sat together around a small table watching the toaster and kettle do their work.

'It's been a funny start to the day,' laughed Tony. His eyebrow fluttered the tissue that was stuck to his forehead. Frank and Sherry burst into laughter.

'Priceless, priceless,' Frank clapped his hands together. 'I have never seen anything like it, it really is a great look, Tony.'

Frank had phoned work five minutes ago, he told them he was going to be late, he had lost his job. It wasn't the first time he had missed his shift and when he thinks back of the chances he had been given, maybe it was understandable. The fact that this time it wasn't his fault didn't help and how ironic that he had come in to buy a lottery ticket to change his life. Little did he know his life was going to change forever, but maybe not in the way he wanted or expected.

The three of them were quiet, they all seemed to be in deep thought. Sherry was thinking about her task, the task her stepfather had forced her to do.

She had flashbacks of the beatings as a small child he gave her when he was drunk. Her mother had been killed in a hit and run when she was three, then as she grew up, he forced her into his bed, she was passed around his friends like a toy. She hated her breasts, her body and her looks. She was 17 but looked in her mid-twenties.

'Listen,' said Tony. 'This is getting stupid; we need to get out of here. Well, you two do, seeing as I work here!'

They all started laughing.

'Shut up and pass the butter,' said Frank. 'I am starving.' With that he leaned over and grabbed the hot toast, put another two pieces of bread in and pushed the handle down, all in one deft move.

'Wow, that was impressive,' said Sherry. 'You a chef or something?'

'Yes, all the best chefs learn that move in Gordon Blue classes,' replied Frank.

As Frank buttered his toast, he thought back of the days when he had ambition, he remembered his first set of chef's knives he bought when he was 13. Chopping and dicing became an art form, he had tried many new and ambitious recipes and loved the feeling of making people happy with food.

'I wanted to open my own restaurant when I was younger,' he said, 'but never had the bollocks to go through with it. That and the money. And the backing of any of my family. Or the missus. Or the dog, I can't understand how I didn't go for it really...'

'Will you wipe that loaf of bread off the side of your mouth away before you talk to me please?' shouted Tony. 'You can't even make toast without spreading it all over your face. What a doughnut.'

'Everyone needs dreams,' said Sherry. 'At least Frank has one he can achieve.'

NUMBERS RUN

'Listen, we need to get out of here. I don't want coffee and toast, I want out!' Frank ran towards the doors and rattled them again. 'Get hold of someone, will you Tony, I need to change my life around and get out!'

'There is no one in the office to do a reset, the lights of the alarm are flashing outside. Someone will see them and contact the police. Just calm down and behave,' said Tony. 'Tell you what we can do, there is a 33-million-pound prize on the lottery tonight, let's pick our lucky numbers and split the money when we win.'

'Lucky numbers. Are you taking the piss?' said Frank. 'I have been doing my lucky numbers for years and all I can say is we need to omit them from anything we pick because they never come up!'

'Come on then,' said Sherry. 'My first number would be number 3, and that's because that's how old I was when I lost my mother and it is the first memory, I have of anything. Not a lucky number but my number.'

Both men for once were quiet, they were both thinking of their mothers and how much influence they had had in their lives.

'Well, my first number would be 13. That's how long I have been married. And I have decided, I don't want to make it to 14,' said Frank.

'My turn then,' said Tony. 'I would say my first number would be 5, no reason just because I like the number 5.'

'Why don't you make it number 4?' said Frank. 'That's the time the news comes on every morning when I set off to work.'

'Why would you even mention another number when we are trying to pick numbers in turn? Are you the biggest jerk ever?' said Tony. 'Now we have to do 3, 4 and 5.'

'Stop, stop, stop,' cried Sherry. 'Let's calm down and start again. We must have a proper reason to pick a number or else it won't work. So, my number is 3. For the reason you know.'

'My number is still 13 because I have still been married for 13 years.'

'My number is going to be 9 because that's the time they are going to come and get us out of here,' said Tony.

'Are you real?' asked Frank. 'What about 4 or 5?'

'Four was never my number. That was yours!' shouted Tony.

'So, it's just the 5 that you're dropping then,' laughed Frank.

'I didn't have a reason to pick that in the first place. So shut the fuck up!'

'Fair enough,' said Sherry. 'My next number would have to be 44. For obvious reasons.'

Frank wrinkled his nose up, 'What you on about... obvious reasons? You said we had to have a reason for a number. So what's yours?'

'Well, you two have been staring at them all morning. I am a 44FF.'

Both the men looked at each other and laughed.

'OK. Good reason, well better than good, a great reason. It's...they... I mean... anyway,' said Frank. 'My next number would be 4. Because that's the time I set off to work and 4 a. m. has to be the worst time in the morning *ever*. Right, it's all down to you, Tony. Go for it.'

'I think I will have to pick number. Hmm. Well, let me see. Five. Because I went to pick it last time but was too scared at what Frank was going say. I am not picking another number. It's number 5.'

MONEY WORRIES

They looked at each other and smiled. For a brief moment, it went quiet and they all seemed to be mesmerised by the six numbers that were written down on the table in front of them.

Tony was thinking of his grandparents that lived in Colledimiezzo, a hilltop village surrounded by countryside. He remembered the cobbled streets that he used to play in and the beautiful smells that surrounded his every movement, the sound of the church bells and the comfort of knowing his father and grandfather were ringing them and one day he would be joining them. That was until his parents left for what they thought would be a better life in the UK, hopefully giving their only son a better education.

They couldn't have been further from the reality of life in Wales. Yes, the countryside was magnificent. The people were friendly. And when the sun shone, it was as good as anywhere in the world. The sun didn't shine for long and the work had dried up.

His father's restaurant had closed. All the family had worked there, father, mother, and himself. The stress had given his father a stroke, his mother spent all her time looking after him. So, all their money worries were on Tony's young shoulders.

He could feel himself beginning to cry just thinking of his mundane life and the struggle his parents were having just trying to stay alive. He spun on his heels and headed for the toilet.

Sherry had different thoughts. Hers were on death. The death of her stepfather and how she could pay a hitman to kill him. Or, better still, give him enough money so he would drink himself to death. She looked at the numbers in front of her, she didn't blink, she just kept thinking of her life without the beatings and perverse acts she was made to do, which somehow had become an everyday way of life.

Her mind drifted to the future. A life with Frank. She didn't know why, but just the thought of his huge frame looking after her and keeping her safe somehow made her feel happy. She didn't even think he was good looking. She didn't know him. What the hell was she thinking? With money, she could do what she wanted when she wanted, the last thing on her mind should be men! She stamped her foot and crossed her arms.

Frank had been deep in thought himself. With his elbow on the table, holding his chin, he had worked out what he was doing with his £11 million. First was to divorce his wife, he was going to give her £1 million, enough for her to live off. He had played the court scene out with the lawyers, they had told him he didn't have to give her anything because of the way he had been treated, but he was a generous man so £1 million was fine.

His small island in the Caribbean where he spent most of his time was secluded and had the perfect temperature all year round. Next to him on his hammock on the beach was the stunning full-bodied topless Sherry. Hang on, he thought. Sherry. What is she doing here? A shot rang out and broke his train of thought. It was Sherry stamping her foot.

'What's rattled your cage?' Frank said to her.

'You. Nothing, I mean. Shut up anyway. Where has Tony gone? We have these numbers, when we going to put them on?'

Tony came running from the toilet. 'I can hear someone outside rattling the doors. We are saved, we are saved!' He let out one of his stupid laughs and they all smiled.

'Hello. Hello. Anyone in there? It's the police. What's going on?'

'Hello police,' Tony shouted back. 'I pushed the alarm button by mistake and can't cancel it. All the doors and windows are dead-bolted or something and I can't get hold of the alarm company.'

'Not a problem,' came the reply. 'We are onto it. Everything OK in there then? There is no robbery. No hostages?'

'No, all is good, there are three of us in here, Frank, Sherry and me. How long do you think it will be?'

'The alarm company are on its way. Hold tight.'

Within ten minutes, the double doors were pushed open by a small bespectacled grey-haired woman holding what looked like a knitting needle.

'There you go, folks, all you needed was to push the button down in the lock there, you should have been told that when they installed the system last month.'

Frank and Sherry turned their gaze to Tony. He had both his hands over his mouth, his eyes wide open, the bit of tissue that was still stuck to his eye started to quiver.

'Shit,' he laughed. 'I can remember now. There was a reset button.'

'What a fucking idiot!' screamed Frank. 'I have lost my job because of you. You fucking Italian prick!'

'You hated that stupid job anyway. I did you a favour. So keep it shut,' replied Tony.

'Will you two calm down?' said Sherry. 'We had a good time, we have been rescued and now it's time to start our new lives... come on, let's have a group hug.'

They all clung to each other and for a few seconds, their individual troubles seemed to melt away. No abuse for Sherry.

No loveless marriage for Frank and no money worries for Tony.

The doors and shutters were reset and light from the outside world shone into the now bright petrol station store. Within seconds Frank was sat in his car wondering what to do next. He turned the key but no response. He wondered if the morning could possibly get any worse. He closed his eyes and lowered his chin to his chest.

GET TO THE RACES

Frank opened his eyes and gave a shiver. When he remembered those events that turned his life around and the way the day could have gone all those months ago, it made him feel sick.

'Honey, are you ready to go? The plane goes in an hour and we are 40 minutes away from the airport,' shouted Sherry.

'On my way, sugar lips, just getting some cash from the safe and putting my lucky pants on. Can you tell Tonto to warm up the limo? I will be there now.'

'Not with those stupid pants again. There is nothing left of them,' Sherry laughed and shook her head.

'Listen, if it wasn't for those pants, we wouldn't be where we are today. Well that, and my good looks and charm.'

Frank ran out of the house down the gravel drive and into the back seat of the limo.

'Drive like the wind, Tonto. We have a plane to catch and a race to win!' He gave Sherry a squeeze and a kiss on the neck. 'Bloody hell woman you get more edible every day.'

'You're not too bad yourself,' she replied.

Sherry was a slimmer version from the first time they met, she had been on a fitness regime and had a breast reduction. Much to Frank's annoyance. She was confident in herself and the memory of her childhood had faded into the past, although it would never be forgotten.

Frank had lost three stone of flab and put on two stone of muscle. His personal trainer had him work out for two hours a day, his chef only cooked him low carb low sugar high protein meals. He had the hair transplant that made him look 15 years younger, his body was firm and chiselled. The size of his shoulders caused his tailor problems, but Frank had never been happier than he was now.

They were on their way to the airport and another exciting week at Ascot races.

'Hey, Tonto. You should have turned left there,' he bellowed out to the driver. There was silence and the darkened glass of the limo raised between the driver and the couple.

'What are you playing at, Tonto?' Frank lowered the glass and noticed the colour of Tonto's neck. It looked very tanned.

Tonto was an albino, one of the reasons Frank gave him the job. He had bright red eyes, he looked very different to anyone he had seen before.

The limo took two sharp right turns and flung Sherry and Frank around like a pair of kittens.

'What the fuck is going on?' screamed Sherry.

The limo screeched to a halt. The silence was broken by a high-pitched laugh. The smoked glass partition came down and there was Tony.

A big smile with dazzling teeth and that little scar on his eyebrow.

'What the fuck are you doing here? You're meant to be in Italy, not Portugal!'

'There's a lot of bad language going on in the back,' replied Tony. 'I just thought we could all go and watch our horse win. I have booked us a villa, a private jet, and transport when we get there... my treat... I also want to see us win millions... again. High Ho Silver away!'

With that, he sped off towards the small private airport less than 4 Km away. As the car drove through the small airport gates, Frank could see an old red Mercedes sports car, roof down, and gleaming in the morning sun, sitting in it was a chauffeur with an old man and woman in the back.

The Limo slowed and Tony started honking the horn. He pulled up to the car and jumped out before the dust settled.

'Mamma, Papa, come, come,' he had his arms open as wide as they could go. His smile was even wider, they all jumped out of the car and the three of them were hugging and kissing each other on the cheeks.

'Frank, Sherry, come and see Mamma and Papa. How good does Papa look now? He has had personal trainers and physio therapists and all types of stuff. We are going to have the best day ever... I am so happy!'

'When was last time you saw your parents? I thought you lived with them,' asked Sherry.

'I do. I saw them this morning. It's just nice to see them again.'

Frank and Sherry looked at each other and smiled, they hoped some day they would have a family as close.

There was a private jet waiting on the tarmac, the stairs were down and, waiting on the top, was an air hostess with a tray of champagne flutes. The group handed their car keys to the airport personnel and they made their way into the plane. As they sat down in the deep leather seats, champagne in hand Frank looked at Tony and raised his glass. No words were spoken just a knowing look between them.

The plane took off and they all sat back.

'Now where would we be if I hadn't messed up those numbers? Can you believe our luck?' said Tony.

'That's right. Bring this up again. You are lucky that you didn't put our numbers on. You were lucky to have pushed the send button exactly when you did... you were lucky your watch was fast as you only got the lucky dips on with a few minutes to spare. But. You were even luckier that you have a great Mamma and Papa who brought you up to be honest. Isn't that right, Mamma?'

Frank turned to her. She smiled and nodded while reaching out for Tony's head and ruffled his hair.' That's ah my boy…he has always been a good boy' she said in a thick Italian accent.

'Well, I suppose 12 million was enough for me so thought you two could do with a bit. Didn't realize you were going to get together and have 24 million between you!' said Tony.

'And that's why I bought the horse for us all. And pay all the fees, now look at us. When he wins today, that will be six-grade ones in a row. He will go to stud and make us millions every year. Now beat that, my little Italian stallion!'

Sherry turned to Frank. 'Frank... tell me again... why is this race so important for us? I know we like to win, but how can this mean so much money... especially if this is his last race and he goes to stud. What do you mean stud?'

'Well, my beautiful little sugar plum. That horse will have a life that only us stallions can dream about. Just doing what we do best, day in, day out and getting paid an extremely high amount of money every time. Now do you understand?'

'If that's how you explain things, no wonder she doesn't understand,' said Tony.

'They bring him mares to service. You know... get pregnant. We get paid a lot of money and this happens two or three times a day if we are lucky. The better the baby horses do when they start racing, the more money we can charge for his services. Now does that make more sense than the Big Yins explanation?'

Sherry started laughing. 'So he gets paid for shagging. Two or three times a day. What a job!'

The flight took nearly two and a half hours, but seemed to be over much quicker, they all spent their time laughing and telling tales of what they had been doing since the last time they had seen each other, which was only three weeks earlier.

The plane landed in a small airport just outside London.

'Okay everyone, follow me. Tony the planner, best friend, and best son ever will now get you to the races in style.' He pointed to a helicopter and limousine. 'Now Mamma and Papa, don't worry you can go in the limousine. I know you wouldn't get in the helicopter; they will show you where we are when you get to the Races. Okay driver, these are very special VIP passengers. You make sure you look after them.' He gave the chauffeur a £100 tip.

'Yes sir. Will do… thank you.' The driver helped them both into the Humber limo, it was nice and high and easier to get into than the normal ones. Tony had thought of everything. After many hugs and kisses from their doting son, their limo drove off.

'Come on you pair of love birds, we have a scenic trip around London then off to the races.'

FLY OR DRIVE?

'Frank, Tony, I don't think I will like it. I want to go in the car... it's too noisy and windy. Frank, please don't make me go.'

'It's alright, I will be there right with you and if you want to come down, we will. Right, Tony?'

'Right Frank,' and he winked with his scarred eyebrow.

They all got in buckled up and put their headphones on. As they took off, Sherry gripped Frank's hand and closed her eyes. It was like floating on air. She opened her eyes after a few moments. They were high above the ground, the sky was clear and the views were spectacular.

'I love it. I love it.' Sherry's eyes were wide open, her smile was huge, and she had stopped gripping Frank's hand so tightly.

Frank looked into Sherry's eyes and smiled, he put his hand on Tony's shoulder looked over to him and said, 'Who would have thought it? Us three in this position...how funny is life?'

Tony smiled and raised his eyebrows; one was still offline. The three of them laughed, they really had found friendship.

The helicopter landed at Ascot races. As they got out, the crowds were looking and wondered who they were, Sherry felt like a film star and Frank looked and felt like a bodyguard with his two tiny VIP guests in tow... his stride lengthened and within a few moments, Sherry and Tony were left in his dust.

'Hang on you bloody emu striding lanky buffoon. Wait for us... you don't even know where you're supposed to be going!'

'Oh yes. You got a point there. But you better hurry up before anyone thinks you're a small jockey and puts you on a horse.

Sorry, Sherry, I forgot about your little tiny trotters. Come here,' with that Frank had run back and scooped her up carrying her like a child, her dress had ridden up and she was showing her bare ass to the onlooking cheering crowd.

'Put me down, you big twit. I got no knickers on. What you mean trotters!' she kissed his neck and grabbed his ear. 'Now put me down.'

He placed her gently on the ground and patted her bum.

'When you two have stopped messing around, you need to follow me. Mamma and Papa will be here soon. We need to be there before them,' said Tony.

Tony led them to the owners' private bar, they had a table booked with a very large ice bucket filled with four bottles of champagne.

'So. They only brought your drinks out then, Franky big bollocks!' said Tony.

'Good one, Tony Baloney. Never heard that one before. You can suck on the cork if you can pick it up with your teeny tiny hands and fingers.'

They laughed and started pouring the drinks. Within twenty minutes, Tony's mother and father had arrived the party was complete, now the wait for the last race began.

They all sat quietly compared to the mayhem going around them, after every race the connections of the winning and placed horses would mingle with the rest of the owners, bad luck stories and unlucky bets were the order of the day.

It was ten minutes before the off time and they made their way to the viewing area. As they took their seats, no one spoke, Frank and Sherry held hands while Tony sat between his mother and father and talked in Italian. The minutes leading up to the race seemed to last for hours and everything slowed down. Knowing that a racehorse could be so important didn't seem right. They all had millions in the bank, but this would mean so many more. Is it true, the more you have the more you want?

The race had begun, it was over in a flash. Their horse won by nine lengths in a record time. His stud fees would be millions, by the time they had collected the trophy and had the photos taken, Tony's mother and father were ready to leave.

'Tony, we are so tired now it has been a long day. Where are we staying tonight?' his mother asked.

'You wait until you see it, Mamma, it has an indoor swimming pool and ten bedrooms! Come Papa, I will take you to the limo. Frank, Sherry, I will come back for you, I won't be long.'

'No Tony, we will come with you in the helicopter, it will be good. We have never been in one… we want to all go together. Sherry said she liked it. Come.'

The five of them got to the helicopter sharing plans for the future on the way.

Less than an hour later, the local TV was filming live from the racecourse.

'Breaking news from the Ascot Racecourse,' the news anchor said, looking straight into the camera, in front of a mass of flames and smoke. Her voice was briefly interrupted by the sound of ambulances and fire engines. 'A few minutes after taking off, the helicopter lost control and crashed into the crowd,' she said. 'The screams and panic flooded the faces of the unhurt mass.' She turned towards the unfolding scene in the background. 'Flames and broken parts rained around the throng and maimed everyone they touched. The six occupants of the helicopter died on impact. Forty-four people and one horse have died this afternoon.'

PENSION DAY

The day began just like any other, Frank a 6ft 6in toned and bronzed giant of a man spread his arms and legs open and closed in his 7ft square waterbed. He reached for the remote that operated the household gadgets and opened the curtains. the sun shone brightly, and he blinked a few times to get used to the light.

'What's the time? Hello Alexa. What is the time?'

'The time is five-thirty in the morning.'

'What have I got planned for today?'

'You have a meeting with your personal trainer at nine and dinner booked for seven in Tony's.'

'Thank you, Alexa. Can you play the best of Bob Dylan starting with Buckets of Rain? Louder. Louder.'

The music blasted out as Frank made his way to his en-suite. He had been on his own now for nearly 2 years. His wife had been in a fatal car accident along with Charlie. He didn't know the full story, but they crashed on their way from a work's weekend away. Police say it was a tragic accident that may have been caused by a wasp stinging the driver. Nothing was confirmed.

He could never understand how she climbed the corporate ladder so fast; she had only worked there for three years, yet she had already been made a director. She and Charlie used to do karaoke together, he was a Mick Hucknall look-alike with a mass of curly ginger hair. The women loved him.

It meant that Frank had given his job up when all the insurances paid out. It totalled nearly three million cash along with a monthly pension from her firm. She was high up in the company and it all came to Frank. There wasn't a day go by that he didn't think of them both. The two people he knew best, both gone.

Frank showered and changed; he checked his bank balance on his phone. Eight thousand pounds deposited from his wife's pension, he had never been so wealthy and so poor. He opened the side door into the garage, locked it behind him and jumped into his vintage Mercedes. The roof was down. He started the engine and sat there for a while.

Inside the double garage, the carbon monoxide started to build up and he thought how easy it would be to just sit there and meet his wife and best friend again. He started to cry and bowed his head. As he looked up into the rear-view mirror, he looked at himself. He hadn't felt so low since the call about the accident.

'Bollocks!' he shouted and pushed the remote for the garage doors. As they opened, the sun shone through the smoke from the car. He drove out of the garage and into the sun, the warm hit his face, his tears stopped, and the wind blew his thoughts away.

He parked outside the gym and wandered in through the double doors. As he walked past the full-length double mirrors, he spun around and flexed his muscles.

'Looking good freaky man... how they hanging?' It was Tony, his new business partner, and old gym buddy.

'Hey midget boy... how is everything at the restaurant? Already for tonight?'

With money Frank had received from his wife's death, he had invested in a restaurant for Tony and his parents, they had great cooking skills, but nil business skills. Frank was only too happy to invest, at least something good may come from his wife's death.

'Listen, Frank, I got to thank you for doing this. It has affected the whole family... and in a good way, not the way you normally affect people. With your huge head, massive hands, and gigantic frame.' They both laughed, Frank picked him up and shook him like a rag doll.

'Stop it... stop it... you're fucking killing me... I can't breathe...' Tony gasped.

'Grow up you little Italian work-shy Fop,' replied Frank. He placed him down gently to the floor.

'Work-shy... work-shy. You cheeky twat, I have been doing twenty-hour days to get that restaurant ready. Rebuilding the kitchen. Stocking the bar.'

Frank butted in. 'Alright calm down calm down, I was only joking.'

Tony carried on 'Interviewing new bar staff and waitresses. Now that's a job I DON'T mind doing. I can tell you.'

'Bar staff and waitresses. What the hell will you be doing then there's only enough room for five people?' said Frank.

'Five people my arse. More like fifty-five. Anyway, I have found my new wife. Sherry. Oh my God, wait until you see her tonight she is U N B E R L E A V A B U B B L E.' Tony spelled the words out to Frank, very slowly.

'You really are a prize chump... you can't even spell it, let alone say it!' replied Frank. 'Now come on let's get into the gym I have a very, very, busy day.'

They walked side by side into the changing rooms like a Dad with his young son.

SPAGHETTI BOLOGNESE

Frank pressed re-dial on his phone. He had a missed call off Tony.

'Frank, Tony here. We are in a right mess; we need you at the restaurant to give us a hand. Can you come as quick as you can, bring your clothes here and change the flat if you want, please? We need your monkey-length arms and gigantic clasping fingers.'

Frank drove the three miles to the restaurant and burst through the door. The shock of seeing the man-mountain gave Tony's mother a fright and the tray of clean dishes she was about to lay out on the tables went three foot in the air and smashed on the terracotta tiled flooring.

'Perché è così grande? Cosa c'è di sbagliato nell'uomo che deve entrare così? she cried.

'Mamma, mamma. What's happened?' Tony came running in from the kitchen. 'Oh, it's only Frank making his usual burst through the door the circus is in town entrance!'

'You know, for a little Italian pony, you really do have a winning way with your customers. Now what's all the panic and fuss you need my help with?'

'Well, for a start,' said Tony, 'you can clear that mess up,' and pointed to the million pieces of white china spread everywhere.

'Yes, good thinking garlic breath, get the biggest man in here to clean the floor,' replied Frank.

'Leave that to me,' said a voice from nowhere.

Frank turned around and looked down on an angel. She was looking up at him wide-eyed and smiling.

'Great,' said Tony. 'Frank meet Sherry. Sherry meet Frank. Take that smug look off your face, Franky boy, and give me a hand in the kitchen. Come on, come on. There look reach up and get those big tins of tomatoes, I told you not to put them up there, who else but a giant could get them back down?'

Frank reached up and got a 5kg tin down with one in each hand.

'Wow. You know what they say about men with big hands.'

Sherry had walked into the kitchen.

'Yes,' said Tony. 'They need big gloves... anyway, with the size of his sausage fingers, there's not much else he can do apart from shovelling sand on a building site.'

'Yes, yes, yes the old ones are the best,' replied Frank. 'At least I don't have to go shopping at the children's section of Tesco. Anyway was there anything else mini-me needed? I do have to get changed you know.'

'No, your work here is done, Gigantor, you can go and do your hair and makeup and put your new dress on... but don't wear those high heels you have trouble getting through doors now!' Tony gave one of his weasel laughs and as he turned to look at Sherry.

Frank grabbed him around the waist and pretended to lift him up on the shelf. It caught Tony by surprise, as he twisted around to look at Frank, he caught his eye on the large copper handle of the cooking pot on the shelf.

'What the fuck... look what you've done now... put me down, you stupid big hairy ape. I'm bleeding,' Tony had blood trickling down his face and onto his chef's whites.

Sherry grabbed some kitchen towels and pressed them on the cut.

'What the! Are you taking the piss?' asked Tony. 'Can you try and hurt me any more than monkey boy just did? Are you two a double act…'

'Stop moaning,' replied Sherry. 'I am trying to stop the blood, here you press down on it. Keep the pressure on I will get a plaster.' She looked into her handbag, which her mother had lent her and started pulling out all sorts of everything, as it started spilling on the floor.

The two men standing behind her looked at each other and pursed their lips together, 'Oh, traveling light tonight?' they said in unison.

Sherry looked around just as she found the rather large container of plasters, 'Do you want me to stop that bleeding or not? It's my mother's bag and she happens to have a lot of must-have stuff to carry around, we both have the same bag and I picked up the wrong one. Come here, you big baby.'

Tony hung his head and leaned forward so she could reach his bleeding eyebrow.

'That, my little Italian stallion, is going to leave a scar,' said Sherry. 'You may have to go to the hospital if this doesn't stick to your rather thick eyebrow.'

'It goes with his thick head,' said Frank. 'He can't go anywhere anyway, we need to open in 20 minutes, it has to work. Let me shave it off and it *will* work. I'm sure.'

'You can piss off!' screamed Tony. 'I will look like an idiot for months with one shaved eyebrow.'

'Months,' said Frank. 'You always look like an idiot... with or without eyebrows. Now get the biggest plaster you have there, nurse Sherry, and sort monkey boy out.'

Sherry applied what looked like a small nappy on the cut and, as she pressed it to his eyebrow, Frank held the back of his head and took the strain.

'Are you two fucking serious?' yelled Tony. 'You're squeezing my head flat!'

'There, all done.' Sherry stepped back and burst into laughter. As Tony turned around to look at himself in the mirror, Frank had put both his hands over his mouth and his shoulders were shaking uncontrollably.

'Oh, for God's sake, this is a fucking joke!' shouted Tony, half his face seemed to be covered by a plaster. 'Come on, come on. Everyone, we have 15 minutes to get ready. Forget about my face, for now, we need to get to work!' he clapped his hands and everyone seemed to know what to do.'

For a small man he knew how to get people motivated and he was respected.

The next six hours went like clockwork, it couldn't have gone any better, the tables were full all night, the food came out of the kitchen without a single problem, all the staff and family seemed to bond together and enjoyed being together. Frank stood in the corner of the room and looked on as the last customers left. His thoughts were on his wife and the hole that she had left in his life. She would have loved tonight. He had no idea she had been ready to leave him for his best friend, sometimes it's better not to know the truth. He kept staring at the closed doors, he felt a movement close by as he turned, he looked at Sherry who had two glasses of champagne in her hand.

'Here you are boss. Compliments of the house. Well, you, really.'

Frank laughed. 'Thank you very much,' he said. 'Just what the doctor ordered. Tony... Mamma... Papa. Everyone... lock that door and get a glass. What a great night, everyone. What a great night, let's hope we never forget it. Cheers, everyone!'

As they raised their glasses in the air, the smiles on their faces were priceless. Frank looked at Tony who smiled and gave him a wink while nodding towards Sherry. Tony's Mamma and Papa went over and hugged Tony.

Frank turned to look at Sherry and they automatically started hugging, which somehow turned into a kiss, the sweet taste of champagne on their lips and mouths kept the kiss together.

The room was silent and everyone's eyes were on the couple in the corner embracing. Since Frank's wife had died, he had never even touched another woman, let alone kiss one.

Tony was both crushed and happy. His friend and business partner for the first time in years may have found someone to share time with.

'Put her down you, big buffoon,' Tony yelled. Everyone clapped, whooped and whistled.

Frank felt bad, his thoughts were on his dead wife, not Sherry.

'That's embarrassing,' she said. 'Sorry, everything's just... I don't know. It seemed right somehow.'

'Yes, yes I know what you mean,' replied Frank. 'I'm sorry too.'

They both looked at each other and fell silent.

'Well, I'm not that sorry,' Sherry blurted out and she grabbed Frank's neck and pulled him down to her height she kissed him again.

The days tripped into weeks, the weeks into months. Frank had heard all about Sherry's life, a life of running and hiding with her mother from her violent stepfather, a stepfather who would not accept they had left. Unbelievably he also had been killed in a car crash, the difference being it was a relief for Sherry. As they became closer, Frank's memories for his wife faded but were never forgotten. Sherry could feel that he hadn't given himself to her, they spent every waking hour together, Frank even spent his nights in the restaurant helping behind the bar and just making a nuisance of himself, he drove Sherry home to her mother every night and picked her up in the morning.

LIVING TOGETHER

'Come on… come on we are going to be late!' Frank was banging on Tony's front door.

'All right, all right, keep your wig on, it's not that late,' replied Tony. 'Come on in… Sherry come on.' Sherry was waiting in the taxi.

'No… no… no, stay there, Sherry. For fuck's sake Tony, why aren't you ready? Why do you always have to be last when we are going out?'

'Listen, you big hairy gorilla, I have to keep to my beauty regime. It takes time to look this good.'

'Get up earlier then, you prick,' replied Frank. 'We are off, if you don't follow me out this door now, we are leaving without you.'

'Well tough shit, big boy. I am ready. So get your arse into gear and get out of my house!'

They both pilled out of the house laughing as they jumped into the taxi.

'Drive like the wind, Tonto. We have a day at the races to get to,' Frank yelled at the driver. He held his hand out and Sherry took it eagerly, she looked into his eyes and time stood still.

It was a Saturday and the M4 traffic was heavy, Sherry sat in the back leaning into Frank's chest, her eyes closed and her thoughts on marriage and children.

Frank had a copy of the racing post and studied the form. Marking off horses with his pen, circling jockeys, underlining trainers. He lent back, 'Well, there you go... I fancy every horse in every race. What the fuck we supposed to do? Every horse is a champion or won its last 20 races or has my favourite jockey trained by my lucky trainer.'

'Oh baby. Don't stress. Let me pick them,' said Sherry.

Tony spun around from the front seat nearly garrotting himself with the seat belt 'Wait! Wait. wait... DO NOT say a word. DO NOT mention any numbers... colours... lucky names. Neighbour's cat's owners' favourite foods. I need to pick my horses without my mind being clouded by your blabbing.'

'Oooh, someone's tired!' replied Sherry. 'Number 4, number 6, numb...'

'Honestly you have to shut up,' cried Tony. 'Will you tell her Frank? If she doesn't stop, I am going home!'

'Anyone else got that feeling this has happened before? I have goose bumps all over,' said Frank.

'You mean De Ja fucking vu, don't you, pea brain? And no, this hasn't happened before, we have never gone to Ascot.'

'Not that you prat. The picking out of numbers. I got a 5, 4, 22.'

Tony held his head in his hands and rubbed his face. 'Now you're doing it! I give up... this is a joke, we may as well close our eyes and use a pin!'

'I have a pin,' Sherry said, 'but I like the idea of picking our favourite numbers, can we do that Frank? Please, please, please,' she rubbed the inside of his leg and gave him a wicked smile.

'We certainly can, sugar lips. What's your first number?'

'Wow, that was easy,' she said. 'I will have to remember that tactic to get my way. Right, for the first race I want number 3, not sure why. It just popped into my head.'

'Well that's a good enough reason,' said Frank and he cupped her face in his giant hands and kissed her full on the lips. My first number is lucky 13 for the second race. Hang on, how many runners in the second, dozy bollocks?'

'I presume you are talking to me,' said Tony. 'There are eighteen runners in the second. The one you picked is 28-1, it's called I Don't Have a Chance in Hellsville! Sherry's horse is 16-1 that one is called You Got Hopes and One of them is Bob. This my giant friend, is a waste of time and money.'

'OK,' said Sherry. 'Me and lover boy will do it. All that lovely money will be ours. All ours,' she was rubbing her hands together and cackling like a witch.

'You're both fucking mad and deserve each other,' he laughed. 'Go on then, race 3, I am going for... number... 5... no, 9. Yes, number 9.'

'What? Why would you change it? What if number 5 wins that race? We will always be wondering. We will have to do both of them,' said Frank.

'Yes. W h a t e V E R!' came the reply. 'We can do number 5 for race 4 instead.'

'That's it,' said Frank. 'Let's forget it, we can just all do our horses and bet on our own, it was all getting too weird, I swear that had all happened before. Now can we all please keep shtum we only have... how long before we get there, driver?'

'Not long now about fifteen minutes,' came the reply.

'Cheers driver. There you two... fifteen minutes to touch down and glory. I have in the palm of my hand the winners of every race. The prize. Two million of your British pounds!' Frank was rolling his hands over each other and laughing loudly.

'W h a t... a... l o a d... of... r u b b i s h,' sang Tony. 'I have the winner of every race and the two-million-pound prize will be mine! All mine.'

'What a pair of dopey dimwits. If anyone knows anything, there can be only one person that could perform such a miracle on such a day and that is a *woman*. And that woman is ddaddaaddadarr... me! I have all the winners. Now what am I supposed to do with them? How do you put a bet on to win two million British pounds?'

There was quiet in the car.

'OK... what I suggest is you both give me your selections, I will see which ones we have picked the same, then I will perm them all in trebles. There are eight races so the minimum will be fifty-six trebles, and that's if we have picked all the same horses, maybe not a good idea we can do the tote placepot as well. And let's do the ITV 7 too... how much money do we want to spend?'

Sherry and Tony just looked at each other as Frank held out his hands for their selections.

'What the fuck are you talking about?' said Sherry, Tony and the driver.

'Just give me your picks. I, the great mighty Frank, will pay for your day out. Frank the man of mystery. Frank the giver to the poor. Frank the Fabulous.'

'OK, cut the crap, you huge buffoon. You are not paying for my bets. I the great mighty Tony will pay for...'

'Hang on, hang on,' Sherry butted in, 'let's not go through all that, we are here. And I the great Sherry will gladly accept the offer of a free day out as I have provided all the winners, so I don't care who pays.'

They all bundled out of the car laughing. 'Thanks, driver,' came a unison of voices and they headed towards the hospitality suits. Frank had splashed out and got a private box for them all, but kept it quiet.

'Come on you two, follow me. Over there. Chop chop. Get those little legs working.' Frank was striding towards the private boxes, Tony and Sherry were half running to keep up with him.

'Slow down, baby. I can't keep up… Oh… I've broken my heel now. Baby. Stop!'

Frank stopped immediately, in full stride, like a statue, arms frozen in full swing.

'Why do you always do that? Whenever we go anywhere, you have to shoot off like a bullet with your giant feet and crazy leg strides. How am I supposed to keep up? 'I'm the same,' said Sherry.

'Come on, the pair of you. You're not children. You're both nearly fully-grown adults!'

By this time, they had caught up with him and gave him a smack on the bum.

'You better be careful what you say, big boy, unless you want to sleep on the sofa.' Sherry caught his outstretched hand and pulled him towards her, a little spark of electricity went through their fingers and they looked into each other's eyes.

'Will you two give it a rest?' said Tony. 'Where are we heading for anyway? The grandstand is over there,' he pointed over to his right.

'No cheap seats for us my little furry friend we are up with the gods.' He pointed to the top of the grandstand. 'Come on, let's go... '

As they opened the door to their private box, they were greeted with a free bar and a table full of sandwiches and snacks.

'YES. I love it!' screeched Tony. 'I need a drink and some fancy pants food.'

Sherry put her arms around Frank's waist and buried her head in his chest. 'You shouldn't throw your money away on this type of thing... but it is nice. Tony, get me a glass of champers while your there.'

'Yes, and I'll have one as well please, young man.'

The three of them looked out at the scene below, a cold glass of champagne in one hand and a pastry in the other. They just sat and stared and drank in the atmosphere. For what seemed like hours, they were silent.

'Right,' bellowed Frank, to which both Sherry and Tony spilled their drinks over themselves with fright.

'You really are a fucking idiot. Look at this shirt now... and my trousers.'

'Oh, shut up. It will soon dry. Now I have a lot of work to do, give me those horse fancies of yours and we can win the jackpot!'

Both Sherry and Tony handed their tips to Franks huge outstretched hand, he got his pen out and started work, in a matter of minutes he had filled in different slips of paper, he stood up and left the room.

'What a big buffoon. I bet we don't get one winner,' Tony shouted after him as he let the door close behind him. 'Just me and you then sweetheart,' he said in his best Humphry Bogart voice to Sherry.

After watching the first six winners, they were all very quiet and laughter had turned to a slight panic.

'I can't cope with this. Do you know how much we could win? Well... do you?' Tony's voice was rather high pitched and slightly squeaky.

'Yes, my little Italian powder puff. But you don't. Have I got a surprise for you both? I have in my top pocket nine. Yes, nine. I repeat nine...' his both hands were raised in the air with nine fingers outstretched.

'Get on with it, you big Yeti. Nine what?' said Tony. Sherry just rolled her eyes and gave Frank a look. That look that Frank loved to get from her. He had fallen in love and couldn't believe his luck.

'Come here,' he grabbed her by her waist and kissed her on the lips.

'Oh, for fuck's sake. Give me a break.'

As Tony turned away, the waitress caught his eye and smiled. Tony smiled back and went to get another champagne. As he got close and held his hand out for the glass, he spun around to face Frank. 'Hang on, nine? Nine what? Put her down and finish off your sentence.'

'Yes. here in my top pocket I have nine. Yes, nine. I...'

'Bollocks to it... you yet again have gone too far with your stupid dustbin lid-sized, giant sausage fingers attached to dinner plate hands sticking them up like a load of turbine-powered windmills. Nine fucking what?'

'As I was saying. In my top pocket.'

'Baby... please tell me what you have nine of.' Sherry looked at him doe-eyed.

'Nine betting slips. Not one. Not two.'

'OK, I get it, nine. What is on your said betting slips? You have the one that we are sharing. What else have you bet on?' asked Tony.

'No... you don't understand... the maximum we could win on one ticket is a million. I have placed the same bets on all nine tickets. That's three tickets each. A possible three million pounds each. What you say now, big bollocks?'

'Oh my god. I feel sick...' Tony ran over to Frank and flung his arms around his neck.

'Calm down... calm down, we have another two races to go, but the trebles we have at the moment come to loads-a-money, let alone the four timers and five timers, and obviously the one six timer...'

Sherry stopped him from talking with a huge kiss on the lips. 'I don't know what you're saying, but I want to marry you.'

Tony was still hanging on to Frank's neck, he was about an inch away from Sherry's face. They had both stopped breathing. Frank's eyes welled up and a tear rolled down his cheek. He put his arms around them both and stood up. 'Yes... yes, let's get married. I do love you, Sherry. We will go to... I don't know. Anywhere...'

In all the confusion, kissing and clinking of champagne flutes, the seventh race had run.

'Frank, Frank... what number did we do in the seventh raced? I hope it was number 7. Tell me it's number 7. It has to be number 7. Look at the photo finish.' Tony stood looking up at Frank back at the freeze-frame on the huge screen outside and back to Frank. 'Well, what was the horse's number?'

'Luckily for you, me and Sherry it was number one. NUMBER. O. N. E.' He was holding his arms high in the air and jumping on the spot. 'We have nearly done it. That is not a seven it's a one. Look. look... the cloth has ridden up. Look at the colours of the jockey.'

The three of them were jumping up and down like school kids, Frank picked them both up under his arms and spun them around.

'Oh my God. Oh my God... what's the last horse? What did you pick?' asked Tony.

'Well, believe it or not, we all picked the same horse. Number 1... the only favourite all day that we picked, he has won its last six races. All group ones. It *has* to win. My god, we have a chance of doing this. Can you believe it! No more worries about anything, we can really start living! Sherry, we can have such a life together if this horse wins.'

After the three of them stopped looking at the tickets and checking the results over and over again, the tension was unbearable, Tony was physically sick and as it dawned on him what this would mean for his family and how he could help his mother and father. The pressure gave him a thumping in his head he had never experienced.

Frank just held hands with Sherry, his stomach was churning. His mind racing, working out ideas and investments, they would never need to struggle again. Where they would live. All resting on a stupid horse race.

Sherry sat and had her marriage plans going through her head, she had planned her wedding day since she could remember. With horse-drawn carriage, a choir and jazz band playing in the afternoon, she didn't even think about the race and she didn't feel nervous.

The race was off. All the horses ran together in a bunch. Their horse was second to last with only two furlongs to go, there was a wall of horses in his way, with one crack of his whip, his jockey found a gap on the rails and in three strides, he went clear of the rest of the field, as the finish line came up he was six lengths clear and pulling away. The crowd went mad... Frank, Sherry and Tony were screaming, the feelings were beyond anything they had ever experienced.

As they left the racecourse, their heads seemed to be buzzing with the noise of the crowd and the bubbles of the champagne.

Could the lives of good people always be destined to succeed? Is success measured by the amount of money there is in your bank account or the lives you have touched along your journey?

They all held hands and smiled.

The helicopter crashed into the crowd the screams and panic flooded the faces of the unhurt mass. Flames and broken parts rained around the throng and maimed everyone they touched.

Frank had Sherry in his arms when they were found, a burnt twisted fused skeleton that couldn't be identified. The thought was that it was a father and daughter. Tony's face had been cut in two by the blades of the helicopter, he had been identified by the scar on his eye. Forty-four people and one horse had died that afternoon, the horse that had won them their new lives, seventeen could not be identified because of the heat from the aviation fuel.

The money they had won was never claimed, Frank had the burnt tickets in his pocket.

Tony's father had another stroke when he heard the news and died shortly after, his mother died holding his hand moments later.

Happier days?

The day began just like any other. Frank, a 6ft 6in balding security guard was being woken by the shrill of his alarm clock. It was dark, it was raining; he hated this time of the day. He felt like a drone that no one knew even existed. His wife of 13 years, Claire, beside him, rolled over and muttered something under her breath about the fantastic night they had. She put her arms around him. He felt great.

As Frank sat on the edge of the bed, he bent over to put his socks on, he could feel his wife's hand on his back. 'Come back to bed. Just for five minutes.'

'Crap,' he muttered. 'I can't be late again, sugar tits; we have a big day today.'

'Shut up, baby. Don't go to work,' said Claire.

'That suits me fine,' said Frank, 'but I need to go. I will be back tonight.'

He put his other sock on and reached for his underpants, they weren't there. He smiled. they must still be downstairs after Claire had jumped on him as soon as he had walked through the door, it had been their wedding anniversary and she gave him a present he wouldn't forget. He reached into his divan bed and pulled out a pair of baggy Y fronts. He hopped slightly to get his legs in, as he reached for his jeans that were hanging on the back of the chair, he leaned forward letting out a high pitched squeaky wet one.

'Baby, you are an idiot!' screamed Claire. She laughed as she hid her nose under the duvet.

'Sorry. Love you, baby,' replied Frank.

He grabbed his Welsh rugby top and headed off to the bathroom. After a quick brush of his teeth and a wash, Frank headed off downstairs.

Breakfast was a bowl of cereals, no sugar and low-fat milk. Mm lovely, he thought, this diabetes was getting him down, but who would want to listen to his moaning?

The stiff front door screeched as he opened it and made his way down the damp dark path to his rusty 15-year old Volvo.

The car started the first time. Wow, he thought, miracles will never cease.

On went the lights, radio, and the blower, the windscreen slowly cleared, and the news came on. It was 4 a. m. The same 4 a. m. as it was yesterday and the day before and the week before and the month before.

'Not much more of this for me!' he muttered to himself. Bob Dylan came on the radio, Buckets of Rain, one of his favourite songs.

He put the car into drive and started his way to work.

To distract himself, he thought about the special delivery today at work. All that gold arriving for the minting of the commemorative coins. Something different, at least.

Frank stopped to get some bread and a lotto ticket from the garage, toast for dinner, toast for tea, he had to eat regularly to stop himself passing out. But keep his weight down at the same time. Eighteen grams of carbs a slice, what a load of crap.

'Morning Tony, just this loaf today and my lucky numbers on the lotto please. Oh, and a pack of 10 Sterling Super kings.' He had known Tony for over three years. A young Italian who worked the dead shift on account of his terrible acne and fear of women.

'Morning Frankie boy, how they hanging?'

'Close to the floor, thanks for asking,' replied Frank.

'You can have this loaf. I was going to chuck it out last night but thought of you. You have to be the tightest bloke I know. Tighter than a duck's ass!' His laugh was like a weasel coughing on speed.

'Cheers, big ears,' replied Frank. He took his cigarettes and loaf turned around and came face to face with an angel.

'Hello,' he said. He did a bit of a sidestep and made his way to the door.

'Sorry, don't I know you?' she said. 'Is your name, Frank?'

' Yes, it is. But I am sorry, I don't know you. I think I would have remembered.' His eyes were fixed on her cleavage.

'Well, I am sure we have met,' she said and placed her outspread fingers on her chest.

'Sorry. Sorry, I didn't mean to stare. Bloody hell how embarrassing is this?' He ran his fingers through what he had left of his hair and closed his eyes.

'Don't worry about it,' she said. 'I love looking at them too.' With that she pushed them even further out.

Frank couldn't believe what he was seeing, Tony was standing with his mouth open and hadn't blinked since the girl had walked in.

'I got to go,' said Frank. 'I'm going to be late. Hang on, where is my lottery ticket not that I ever win?' Tony pushed the buttons and gave him the ticket.

'Well, your luck's in today,' she said. 'After I get my pint of milk, you can come to mine for a coffee and crumpets.'

'Not for me thanks,' replied Frank and he reached out for the door. What the hell was going on? he thought. A woman propositioning him. It must be a setup.

He pressed the button on his key fob and the lights flashed. As he reached to open the door, the lights flashed again and the door was locked. He looked at the fob and pushed it. Lights flashed and he quickly opened the door, the alarm went off.

'Shit!' he shouted. Pressing the fob did nothing, he got out, slammed the door and locked it, the alarm stopped.

As he lent back and looked to the sky, he raised his arms and bellowed. 'What the hell is going on?' With that, his ass got grabbed and a sweet voice said, 'I told you, it's your lucky day.' It was the girl from the petrol station.

'Woow,' screamed a startled Frank. 'You gave me a scare. You shouldn't be doing that to strangers, anyway what's your game? You following me?'

'No. As I said, I would like to make you breakfast at my place. I am lonely and need some company.'

'You are having a tin bath. What the hell is your game? I am a very happily married man and if you think I am going to your place you are an idiot, now get lost and leave me be!'

'Listen. Just relax, we are being watched. Do not look around and just listen to me. I need you to come in my car and we need to go back to my hotel room. Just pretend you want me, and I have picked you up. Please. This way no one gets hurt.'

'Fuck off,' replied Frank. 'You are off your head; I need to get to work, now get lost and leave me alone. You need to see a doctor!'

'Listen, they have Claire. They will kill you, me, and her. Just smile and walk to my car. Please, please listen to me, they know all about you.' She took his hand and walked to her car.

Frank was in a daze, what the hell was this girl saying to him? As they reached her car, he stopped. 'I can't do this. How do you know my name and Claire's name? What the fuck is all this about?' He reached for his phone.

'Just get in the car. Now. You are going to get us all killed, put that phone away!'

He got in and sat there for a moment not blinking. She got in beside him and smiled. 'There, not too difficult, was it?'

She drove out of the petrol station towards the hills.

'Listen,' shouted Frank. 'What the fuck is going on?'

'I need to get your pass off. You deliver it to my father... he is going to steal the gold that is being delivered today.'

'My pass gets me nowhere near the gold delivery. You won't get anything!'

'Let me get one thing straight!' shouted Sherry. 'This has nothing to do with me, I am trying to keep alive, my father is a bastard he will kill you both if he can't get what he wants.'

'Both… does he have Claire?'

There was silence.

Frank grabbed the wheel and forced her off the road and onto a muddy patch of grass, the wheels started spinning, the car came to a stop. The driver hanged her head down and started crying.

'Please help me,' she sobbed. 'I had to get you to my hotel room and steal your pass.'

'My pass is no good to anyone, I have no entry to the gold rooms. Please tell me, do you have my wife?'

'No. But if I don't get your pass, I will be in for another beating.'

'Take my fucking pass. Here… now get me back to my car, I need to get to my wife.'

They drove back in silence.

As Frank got out, the girl said, 'Please do not call the police yet, give me a chance to give this to my father. Please I beg you.' She started sobbing again.

'I owe you nothing. Now fuck off and leave me alone!'

Frank ran towards his car, opened the door, inserted the key, and drove off home.

He parked a few doors away and made his way to the back of his house.

After peering through the kitchen window, he saw no sign of life. Quietly he unlocked the door and made his way in. Nothing seemed to be out of place but there appeared to be movement upstairs.

He made his way to the stairs and listened intently more noises. Someone talking. He went back into the kitchen and grabbed a knife. Very slowly he made his way up the stairs, the voices were muffled. They were coming from the bedroom. The door was slightly open, and he peered through the crack, his hand tightening on the handle of the knife.

He could make out the back of his wife riding on the body of a man. A man he knew well. His best friend Charlie. He could make out his mop of ginger hair. Frank's heart stopped, his life had stopped, he dropped the knife and fell to his knees. As he put his hand out to stop himself toppling over, he pushed the door open and fell to the floor.

His loving wife screamed, as she turned and saw what made the noise. Charlie jumped up and looked in horror as the giant of a man got to his feet. There was silence as the two on the bed stared at Frank. Fear had gripped them both. Frank turned and slowly made his way down the stairs, tears streaming from his eyes down his cheeks, numbness in his head and a buzzing in his ears. He felt giddy and confused.

PAIN

The next thing Frank remembered, he was filling his car up with diesel. He was back at the petrol station he had left an hour ago. The tears had dried up now, but the feeling of utter loss was still with him, as he walked into pay, a friendly voice rang out.

'Hey Frank. How they still hanging?'

Frank looked up and tried to speak. His chin started shaking and as he opened his mouth a high-pitched voice came out from within.

'She's a bitch,' he said and tears started down his cheeks again.

'What the fuck...what's happened Frank? Come here, come around the back.' Tony put his arm around Frank's waist and took him into the kitchen behind the counter.

'What's happened? Was it that girl?'

By now Frank was crying uncontrollably, his huge shoulders shaking as he sobbed.

'What did she do Frank? Frank come on tell me we need to sort this out.'

A voice from behind them shouted, 'Here, have your badge back... I'm sorry, I'm sorry I didn't give it to my stepfather. I didn't mean to make you cry. I don't know what to do, I'm sorry honest.'

Tony stood up and knocked his chair backward as he did 'Who the... why the... give me that pass... Here Tony, here, I have it now. Come on, come on, calm down here it is.'

Frank looked up at Tony, he looked so worried. 'It's not the stupid fucking pass,' he bellowed. 'My Claire has been having it off with Charlie. I just caught them!'

'Oh, shit,' said Tony. 'What have you done? My god. What did you do? Do I need to call an ambulance? Come on Frank talk to me!'

'I didn't do anything. I left... I loved that woman. I don't understand what's happening.' His eyes lowered to the floor and he fell silent.

The three of them were silent for what seemed like an eternity. Frank's phone rang. It was Claire, he looked at it and threw it as hard as he could out into the shop. It caught the 'Pay Here' sign and shattered into pieces. The battery struck a red knob under the counter and the screen flew back into the kitchen and struck Tony in the face.

'What the fuck,' screamed Tony. 'My fucking eye! I'm blind. I'm blind!' the blood started streaming down his face...' It's all going dark. 'I'm blind... I'm blind. Call someone!'

Frank got up and ran into the shop, he grabbed some tissues and ran back to Tony. After putting a box of tissue paper on his face and eye, he too noticed it was getting dark.

'What's happening Tony, all the windows and doors are blacking out shutters are coming down?'

The girl had switched the lights on and moved towards Tony. 'Let me look,' she said. 'Wow, that's a bad gash, do you have any super glue? We need to stick it.'

Frank looked at her and shook his head. He ran into the shop and got a tube. 'Here, will this do?'

'Thanks,' and gave him a smile with her eyes. 'Let me see, lift that tissue up a bit, now I need to be quick? I don't want blood everywhere.' With one quick movement, she had opened the glue, damped the wound down and run a small line of glue on the cut. Before the glue had dried, Tony put the tissue back over the cut and pressed down.

'You have just glued that tissue to your face!' shouted Frank. The girl looked at Tony then Frank and they all let out a laugh. 'What a fucking idiot!' laughed Frank.

The shutters were down, and the rooms went dark.

'What the hell is going on here now?' asked Frank.

'Don't panic, don't panic,' said Tony. 'I had training for such an occasion. From one of the most gorgeous trainers I have ever met. I can still see her now. Apparently, she was new. Anywho... I just get this little needle pin thing and place it over here.' He walked over to the front doors, bent over and pressed the button with the needle.

'How's that!' he raised his arms and started doing the moonwalk.

'Well done Tony, well done. Miracles will never cease. And everyone said you would never amount to anything!'

A DAY OUT

Frank woke with the sun streaming on his face, the window was open, and the birds were in full song. He put his arm out and felt the warm soft skin of Sherry. The past 12 months had flown by. He had never thought in a million years he would be living in a small flat in Cardiff with a girl ten years younger and with the body of a porn star.

'Come on, let's not waste the day, shall we go to the races? Ascot is on. The champion of champions, we can catch the train.'

Sherry opened her eyes and gave Frank a warm smile, she had never felt happier, he protected her from her father, her past life was never spoken about. 'Yes, yes, yes, come on let's have a shower together and get ready,' she said.

Within the hour, Frank was on the phone booking a taxi to take them to the train station.

'We don't need a taxi, we can walk it in 10 mins,' said Sherry.

'Yes, I know,' said Frank and laughed. He grabbed her around the waist and squeezed her until she yelped. She loved it when he did that. She nestled her head into his chest, closed her eyes and felt safe.

A horn blasted outside, they both ran down to the front door and burst through it like school kids.

'How they hanging Frankie boy?' shouted the taxi driver. It was Tony.

'What the fuck you doing driving a taxi? And in the day when women can see you?'

'Never mind that. Are you so lazy you couldn't walk to the train station? It's not even a mile away, it's no wonder you're so… tall!' He was going to say fat, but Frank had gone on a diet and lost over three stone in nine months.

'Shut the fuck up!' They both shouted. 'And drive like the wind.' They bundled themselves into the back of the car.

Within two minutes, they were stopped at the traffic light in a queue as long as your arm.

'Tits,' said Frank. Told you we should have walked.

The lights turned green, yet no one moved. 'Toot your horn… toot your horn. Go on Tony.'

The cab radio came on. 'All drivers, all drivers, the train station has been closed due to safety precaution measures. Repeat, train station closed, all roads are being blocked. Please keep clear. Over.'

'CRAP!' They all yelled in unison. 'What we going to do now?' asked Sherry.

Tony turned the car around and started driving away from the city centre and the mayhem.

'Hang on big bollocks,' said Frank. 'What you up to?'

'I, my giant friend, am going to take you back to the circus from whence you came!'

'Hah… good one… especially as that's where you came from midget clown boy,' replied Frank.

'Can you two kids behave?' said Sherry. 'What are we going to do? We are all dressed up with nowhere to go.'

'Trust me Cinderella. I will get you to the ball.' Tony switched on his radio. 'Cab 44 to base cab 44 to base, having trouble with the car so will clock off for today. Over.'

'OK 44. Dim problem… cheers Tony.'

Within minutes they were on the M4 and driving towards Ascot.

The traffic was heavy, there had been a crash at junction 23, they had only been driving for 30 minutes and already Frank was getting inpatient.

'Shit. We are never going to get there. Let me google train times from Newport. No, that's no good not with Cardiff being closed. Hang on, what about getting off at the Coldra and going that way up to Chepstow and over the bridge? Then it's only about an hour or so.'

'Yes, an hour or so if we were in a plane. I can take that route, anything is better than sitting in this crap. Hang on to your hats.' With that, Tony turned onto the hard shoulder and undertook the slowing traffic.

'You will lose your license, you fool,' said Sherry. 'And I don't like it, make him stop, Frank. Please!'

'Too late, here is our turning. Right Chepstow, here we come.'

They flew over the roundabout and through the green lights.

'Told you. Frank the Stupendous has done it again.'

'Frank the fool, you mean. Look at this lot!' Tony pointed to the queue of stopped traffic in front of them.' Did you honestly think you were the only one to think of this?'

Frank gave him a clip across the back of the head. 'Bollocks!' he shouted.

'Don't worry about it, baby. It's not your fault. Aw, come here.' Sherry cuddled him.

'This was supposed to have been a day for you to remember. Now look at it.'

'I will remember it, oh colossal headed yeti. I could have been wor...' Tony was cut off.

'Not you. You fucking clown. My princess. My main squeeze. My true love. My, my. Maybe my. Well, this wasn't what I had in mind, I have a table booked and everything. Look what I am trying to say is...'

'Here we go, there was just a horse in the road. The traffic doesn't look too bad now, we may get there in time you know, you may have pulled it off. I reckon we may get there for the first race,' said Tony.

'OK. Honestly, just shut up for one minute. Turn into that pub car park. I need to get out. Come on, I need to do something.'

The car pulled into a lovely old pub car park, the type with trees surrounded by gravel and flower borders... the car skidded to a stop and Frank opened the door, he ran around and opened Sherry's door, he held her hand and helped her out.

'What are you doing Frank? Do you feel alright?' she said.

He got down on one knee and put his hand into his trouser pocket.

By now Tony had got out of the driver's side and was standing with both hands covering his mouth.

Sherry started crying and before Frank could say anything, she had leapt on him with her arms around his neck, they fell in a heap on the dusty gravel floor. Tony jumped on them both.

'Yahoo, I'm going to be a father!' he yelled. The three of them laughed uncontrollably. The couple that were having a drink sitting on the bench seat froze and watched the scene in front of them.

'They are getting married!' Tony shouted as he stood up and dusted himself off. 'Getting married. I can't believe it.' He was looking over to the couple. They had stood up and raised their glasses 'Congratulations to you both!'

Frank and Sherry had stood up and patted each other down. Frank's huge hand gently brushing Sherry's cheek, he cupped her face and kissed her. As he pulled away, he whispered in her ear, 'Will you marry me?'

' Yes... yes,' she screamed, and they kissed again.

The three of them walked hand in hand towards the pub door. Tony opened it and told Frank and Sherry to sit outside while he got the drinks. A few moments later he came out with an ice bucket, a bottle of champagne and three glasses.

'Here you go my gigantic friend. You can use the bucket.'

Tony passed Frank the drink and sat down at the table, as Frank popped the cork, they all cheered and laughed. They were not sure why, but it seemed the right thing to do. The bubbles overflowed the glasses and spilled onto the table and floor. As the glasses were raised and pushed together, Frank had never been happier. Sherry was already planning the wedding and Tony was wondering if he should have a drink. He was supposed to be driving.

'Cheers everyone. And here is to a new life!'

The day turned into night; they didn't manage to get to the races. The pub had rooms and they stayed the night.

Within three months, Frank and Sherry were married, Tony the best man met his future wife at the reception, she was one of the waitresses. Children came along for both couples and they lived a normal life with its ups and downs, living close together they remain the best of friends.

Frank always wonders what his life might have been had he not found his wife out on that day. A day that changed his life.

Next page

Next page

Next page

Next page

Well that's one version of events

...are there more?

THE END?

Printed in Great Britain
by Amazon